TOYING WITH
DANGER

Books by Drew Stevenson

TOYING WITH
DANGER

A Sarah Capshaw Mystery

Drew Stevenson
Illustrated by Marcy Dunn Ramsey

COBBLEHILL BOOKS
Dutton   New York

Text copyright © 1993 by Drew Stevenson
Illustrations copyright © 1993 by Marcy Dunn Ramsey

Library of Congress Cataloging-in-Publication Data
Stevenson, Drew, date
Toying with danger   a Sarah Capshaw mystery / Drew Stevenson ;
illustrated by Marcy Dunn Ramsey.
p.   cm.
Summary: With her friends, Clark and Frog, Sarah investigates some
mysterious happenings at an isolated farmhouse in the Pennsylvania
woods where an eccentric toy inventor is working on a Frankenstein
monster.
ISBN 0-525-65115-2
[1. Mystery and detective stories.   2. Inventors—Fiction.]   I. Ramsey,
Marcy Dunn, ill.   II. Title.
PZ7.S84725Tq   1993   [Fic]—dc20   92-19325   CIP   AC

Published in the United States by Cobblehill Books,
an affiliate of Dutton Children's Books,
a division of Penguin Books USA Inc.
375 Hudson Street, New York, New York 10014
Printed in the United States of Ameica
First Edition   10   9   8   7   6   5   4   3   2   1

FOR GALE NANCY, MY BEST FRIEND,

AND TOM AND DONNA FAULS,

WITH FOND MEMORIES

OF TRIPLE SUICIDE SUBMARINE SANDWICHES

—D.S.

TO MY DAUGHTER JESSIE,

THE MAD SCULPTRESS!

—M.D.R.

"If a mystery comes up and bites me,
I won't yell 'ouch.' "

—SARAH CAPSHAW

1

SARAH CAPSHAW was grumpy.

"Wilsonburg sure is a boring town," she muttered.

We were sitting in the diner getting ready to eat a late lunch. I didn't say anything as I watched her rearrange the pickles on her hamburger. Everyone is entitled to their opinion. Even if they are putting down my hometown.

"This burger is terrible," she said, wrinkling her nose.

"Hold it right there!" I snapped.

□

Everyone is entitled to their opinion—*unless* they're talking about Lannigan's Miracle Diner which my parents own and operate in downtown Wilsonburg, Pennsylvania. Any opinions I hear about the diner better be good.

"You haven't even taken a bite yet," I said, glaring at her across the booth.

"Sorry," Sarah replied with a sigh. "It's just that the summer is almost half over and we've only had one mystery to solve."

"That's not true," I protested. "Just last week we helped Sue Levy find her missing cat."

"Big deal," Sarah yawned. "It got locked in the neighbor's garden shed."

"And what about Steven Regina's bike?" I went on. "We found out who took it for a ride without telling him."

"The Case of the Missing Bicycle," Sarah snorted after taking a bite of her hamburger. "Maybe they'll make it into an action-packed movie."

I gave up and concentrated on my bowl of chili. I could see there was no cheering Sarah up. Besides, she did have a point. Earlier in the summer we had cracked a big mystery in town. It involved ghostly happenings at old Maplewood Manor, and our investigation uncovered a crime that no one knew had even happened! I figured a case like that comes around once in a lifetime. I should have known then that big mysteries have a way of finding Sarah Capshaw, amateur detective.

"How's that burger, Sarah?" Mabel, the waitress, called from behind the counter.

"Great, as usual," Sarah admitted. "My compliments to the chef."

"Thank you!" Fred McGhee, our grillman, grinned as he raised his spatula in the air. "Chef McGhee, that's me!"

I laughed and looked around the long, narrow room. Even though the lunch rush was over, the diner was still half full. As Mabel disappeared into the kitchen with a pile of dirty dishes, Goldie came out carrying a big tray loaded with steaming food.

"Hey, Goldie!" Big Walt, the truck driver, yelled from his counter stool. "Is all that for me?"

"In your dreams," Goldie giggled.

Each time the kitchen door swung open, I could hear my dad singing from his usual spot by the stove. "Nothing could be finer than owning the Miracle Diner in Wi-i-l-l-son-burg!" At the front door, my mom was leaning on the cash register, talking with Conrad Capshaw, Sarah's grandfather.

□

"Clark Lannigan!" Sarah scolded. "You're not listening to me!"

"True," I admitted. "I was just thinking about how much I love our diner."

"You *should* be thinking up mysteries for us to solve," Sarah pointed out. "Do you want to end up working in this diner for the rest of your life?"

"Yep," I replied smugly.

"So where's Frog?" Sarah asked impatiently. "He was supposed to meet us here half an hour ago."

"There he is," I said, pointing out the window.

My best friend, Frog Fenniman, was standing on the sidewalk, holding a box and talking with Katie Price. Katie is a friend of ours from school, and Frog seemed real interested in what she was saying. When they were done, Frog came inside and joined us.

"Where have you been?" Sarah demanded.

"And what did Katie have to say?" I wondered, knowing full well that she was usually up on the latest gossip.

"I was working on my new invention," Frog said, looking at Sarah.

Then he turned to me. "And Katie was just telling me that Franklin O'Grady and his gang saw a monster!"

☐

2

"A MONSTER?" Sarah cried. "Tell me more."

"It happened last night," Frog explained. "Franklin and his gang were out snooping around the old Harley farm."

"Why would anyone want to snoop around that creepy place?" Mabel wondered as she stopped to take Frog's order.

"Creepy people like Franklin do creepy things," I chuckled.

"I want to know more about this farm," Sarah demanded.

☐

I explained that the old Harley farm is out on Misty Hollow Road. The road runs through the middle of Misty Woods, a deep, dark forest. After Mr. Harley died, the farm sat empty for a long time. No one wanted to buy it. It's the only place on the whole road, and it has to be the loneliest spot in the county.

"And then the mad scientist bought it," Frog piped up.

"Mad scientist?" Sarah exclaimed.

"He's not a mad scientist," I corrected Frog. "He's some kind of inventor."

"You'd have to be *crazy* to live out there alone," Frog argued.

I opened my mouth, and then shut it. I was afraid he just might be right. No one knew much about the man who had bought the Harley farm. According to the rumors that flew from booth to booth around the diner, the new owner was an eccentric inventor. He was living alone out there and didn't want people coming around.

"Get to the monster part," Sarah urged Frog.

"Last night Franklin and his gang were snooping around the farm," Frog went on. "When they saw a light on in the barn, they decided to peek in a window. That's when they saw *it*."

□

Frog paused as Mabel dropped off his cheeseburger.

"Saw *what*?" Sarah almost yelled.

"A Frankenstein monster!" Frog declared. "It was lying on a table, just like in the movies."

"You don't say!" Mabel gasped. "What did those kids do?"

"They took off running," Frog chuckled. "And didn't stop until they were back in town."

I glanced nervously over at Sarah. She was clenching her fists and looking peeved. Franklin O'Grady, of all people, had just had a scary, mysterious adventure and folks were talking about it. The most exciting thing that had happened lately to Sarah Capshaw, amateur detective, was finding a missing cat.

"I know what you're thinking!" I accused her. "But Frog and I aren't going out to any spooky old farm looking for monsters."

"Frog, my brilliant friend," Sarah said, changing the subject. "What's this about an invention?"

"Don't ask," I warned. "His last invention was an ant farm that looked like a *real* farm with barns and stuff."

"So what's wrong with that?" Sarah said. "Sounds cute."

"It was," I replied, "except Frog's ant farm didn't have a lid."

□

"My ants staged a mass escape," Frog said sadly,

"Yeah," I growled. "In *my* bedroom."

"Born free!" Frog began singing. "As free as the wind blows. As free as the grass . . ."

I clamped my hand over his mouth while Sarah began emptying the contents of Frog's box onto the table. There was one large piece of cardboard and a lot of little squares of paper.

"Someday this will be the most popular board game since Monopoly and Trivial Pursuit." Frog beamed proudly as he unfolded the piece of cardboard.

The board had small squares snaking all around it, with words printed in each square. They said things like TAKE A CLUE CARD or PICK A DANGER CARD.

"Each player picks a famous detective to be," Frog explained. "You can choose Sherlock Holmes, Dick Tracy, Miss Marple, Nancy Drew, or Sarah Capshaw. It's called Super-Duper Sleuths."

"Sarah Capshaw?" Sarah's eyes lit up.

"You roll the die and move around the board," Frog went on. "The Clue Cards will help you solve the mystery. But the Danger Cards will get you in trouble and make you miss turns. I still haven't worked out all the details yet."

□

I picked up a Danger Card. It said, "The suspect has just pushed you into the lake. Lose one turn."

"This is *almost* as dumb as an ant farm without a lid," I snorted.

"Well, I like it!" Sarah exclaimed.

"That's just because you're one of his super-duper sleuths," I pointed out.

"And you're not!" Sarah shot back. "Jealous?"

Then she turned and smiled at Frog. It reminded me of a cat smiling at a mouse.

"You know something, Frog?" she said innocently. "If we went out to the Harley farm tonight, you just might get some good ideas for your new game."

"Forget it!" he cried.

"I couldn't have said it better myself," I agreed.

Sarah shrugged her shoulders. "Then I guess I'll just have to go out there by myself."

"Have a nice trip!" Frog snorted.

"Yeah," I hooted. "And don't forget to write!"

□

3

THE SUMMER DUSK was thickening into darkness as Sarah, Frog, and I walked out Route 19 toward Misty Hollow Road. Sarah was wearing her fedora hat over her long, blonde hair. It made her look like a detective in an old movie.

"I can't believe we're doing this," Frog muttered.

"I can't believe we actually thought she'd take no for an answer," I said.

When Sarah Capshaw sniffs a mystery, she's like a human bloodhound. She never gives up.

□

And that included making Frog and me feel so guilty that we finally agreed to go out to the Harley farm with her.

"How do we even know Franklin was telling the truth about this monster stuff?" I grumbled. "He's no George Washington, you know."

"That's what we're going to find out," Sarah answered.

"I just bet you think there's a big fat mystery waiting for us," I said.

"If a mystery comes up and bites me, I won't yell 'ouch.'" The super-duper sleuth grinned.

With each step I felt myself getting madder and madder at Franklin. It was *his* fault we were on our way to the middle of nowhere. For as long as I can remember, Franklin has been a pain in my neck. In my whole body. In the football game of life, Franklin O'Grady is a fumble.

And I wasn't his only victim. Not by a long shot. When Frederick Fenniman was in the third grade, it was Franklin who made him eat a fly. From that day on, Frederick became known as Frog. And, of course, it was Franklin who had borrowed Steven Regina's bike in what Sarah referred to as The Case of the Missing Bicycle.

"So where's this Misty Hollow Road anyway?" Sarah asked.

□

"Just beyond the trailer park," Frog pointed out.

The lights from the neat rows of trailers looked cheerful and inviting. I knew that Misty Hollow Road was anything but that.

"Here it is," Frog said as we left the traffic and lights of the highway and turned down a narrow dirt road.

Misty Hollow Road always seems to be on the verge of being swallowed up by Misty Woods. Old trees with thick, gnarled trunks grow right to its edge. The branches overhead almost form a tunnel, blocking out light from the stars and rising moon.

Even Sarah stopped chattering about mysteries as the sounds of the highway vanished behind us. Only a few lonely crickets and the soft trickle of a brook somewhere in the thicket broke the eerie stillness.

Twenty minutes later, the trees began to thin out as the road cut through the overgrown fields of the old Harley farm.

"There it is," I whispered.

The two-story wooden farmhouse sat back from the road at the end of a long, gravel driveway. A barn and silo loomed behind it. Though the umbrella of moon and stars cast a

□

soft glow on the fields, it only made the house and outbuildings seem more dark and forbidding.

"Nobody's home," Frog said. "Let's go back to town."

"We're not here to pay a social call!" Sarah snapped. "Let's go."

We crept up the driveway and circled the house. An old car was parked in the barnyard, but everything, including the barn beyond, looked dark and deserted.

"We'll peek in one of the windows," Sarah whispered.

She hurried across the barnyard with Frog and me close behind. We gathered around a small window along the side of the barn.

"Can't see a thing," Sarah complained as she pressed her face against the glass. "Let's try the door."

"Door?" Frog and I gulped.

We followed her around the corner to one of the big doors.

"Ready?" she hissed.

Before I could say no, she gently pushed against it. The door slowly swung open. The inside of the barn was black and silent.

"Now can we go?" Frog asked in a trembling voice.

□

Suddenly the barn erupted in bright light. Blinking in shock, we stared at the proof that Franklin had been telling the truth. Lying on a table in the middle of the barn was a Frankenstein monster!

From his greenish skin to his broad chest to the stitches on his face, he looked like something out of a horror movie. Slowly, the creature sat up and turned his head toward us. His eyes snapped open and the look he gave us was evil and terrifying. Then he opened his mouth and roared with fury!

□

4

FROG AND I shrieked and bolted. Sarah didn't shriek, but she *did* bolt. We didn't stop running until we were way down Misty Hollow Road surrounded by woods again.

"We've got to get help!" Frog babbled. "We'll call the police and the National Guard and the Marines and the . . ."

"Pull yourself together," Sarah snapped.

"Frog's right," I said. "You saw that . . . *thing*."

"I saw a lot of things back there," Sarah replied coolly. "And *this* detective is mighty suspicious."

□

"What are you getting at?" Frog demanded. "Are you saying that monster wasn't real?"

"Didn't you see what was all around the barn?" she asked.

"No," I admitted. "I was too . . ."

I was about to say "scared," but stopped myself.

". . . busy looking at the monster," I finished.

"A good detective is always observant," Sarah said in that snooty voice of hers. "That's why *I* noticed that the barn was full of electronic equipment."

"Electronic equipment?" Frog wondered.

"And didn't you tell me," Sarah went on, "that the mysterious man who bought the Harley farm is an *inventor?*"

"I still think he's a mad scientist," Frog argued. "That would explain what we just saw back there."

"What we saw is a *robot*," Sarah explained.

That made sense! Deep down I was having trouble really believing in the monster. And yet I had seen it with my own eyes. Sarah's robot theory was the answer. The monster was real, but it wasn't alive. And a robot would explain all the electronic equipment Sarah had seen inside the barn.

"Wow!" Frog exclaimed. "A mad *inventor* is

□

building killer robot monsters. Before long, they'll take over the whole county!"

"We'll come back tomorrow," Sarah said, ignoring him, "and continue our investigation in the daylight when we can see more."

"I can't," Frog squeaked. "Tomorrow I have to give Churchill a bath."

Churchill is Frog's pet bulldog.

"Anytime you don't want to do something, you give Churchill a bath," Sarah accused. "He's got to be the cleanest dog in the world."

"All right, count me in," Frog finally agreed. "But if that creature turns us into Frankenstein burgers, it's your fault!"

After Misty Hollow Road, little Wilsonburg seemed like a bustling big city. We split up on Main Street and headed for our homes. As I walked the familiar streets, I thought about Sarah. Her real home was down the river in Pittsburgh. She was staying here for the summer with her grandparents while her mom and dad were out of the country on business. Her grandfather was Conrad Capshaw, a well-known lawyer around western Pennsylvania.

Before Sarah came to town, Frog and I would do exciting things like riding the escalators in

□

Caldwell's Department Store. Now we were having terrifying encounters with monsters. What a change!

As usual, my parents had left for the diner by the time I got up the next morning. When I came downstairs, my grandmother was in the living room reading the *Observer-Reporter* newspaper. Grandma stays with my little sister, Clara, while Mom and Dad are working together. Clara was pushing her favorite toy truck across the coffee table. She calls it Mr. Vroom Vroom.

I visited with Grandma for awhile, and then went down to the diner. After I put in my shift, Sarah, Frog, and I headed out to the Harley farm.

In broad daylight, we had to be careful as we crept toward the barn. We used scattered trees and bushes for cover. The old car was still parked in the barnyard, and the farm still seemed deserted. How did we know for sure, though?

We reached the window and peeked in. The Frankenstein monster was still stretched out on the table. Even though we now suspected he wasn't real, he gave me the creeps. Sarah was right about the electronic equipment. It was scattered around the big room.

□

"No one's in there," Sarah said. "Clark, you and I will go in and look around. Frog, you stay here and keep watch."

Before I could complain about not getting picked to be lookout, Sarah pulled me around the corner to the door. Again, it was unlocked and we slipped inside. The barn was cool and smelled faintly of hay.

We tiptoed toward the monster as if we were afraid of waking him. I held my breath as Sarah reached out to touch him. No sooner had her fingers grazed his huge arm than a tapping sound made us jump back. We looked over at the window and saw Frog frantically waving at us.

"Someone must be coming!" Sarah gasped. "Hide!"

5

WE RAN TOWARD a door at the back of the barn. I was hoping it led outside, but it was locked.

"The hayloft!" I pointed.

We turned and ran back toward the front door where we entered. There was a wooden ladder, and the top of the ladder was attached to a loft overlooking the floor of the barn. We scrambled up the rungs as fast as we could and just made it.

No sooner did we reach the platform than we heard the door opening. A second later, the

□

lights of the barn came on. We crawled to the edge of the loft and peered down. An older man was walking up to the monster. His long, curly hair looked like it hadn't seen a comb in months. He was smoking a pipe and wearing a white lab coat with tools stuffed in every pocket.

As my gaze circled the barn, I could see that it was set up like a workshop. Along with the electronic equipment, there were drafting tables, worktables, and shelves filled with technical-looking books. There were also cabinets filled with tools and wires, and cables snaking across the floor.

The man in the lab coat took a screwdriver and began to tinker with Frankenstein's chest. A minute later, he opened a large panel, exposing the monster's insides. From our perch, I could see that Sarah was right. The monster was a robot filled with all kinds of wires and circuits.

The man leaned over the monster and talked to himself as he worked. A few minutes later, we heard a vehicle pull up outside and a door slamming. The man looked up from the monster as another man entered the barn.

The newcomer was young and handsome, with blond hair and plenty of muscles. He was wearing a T-shirt and jeans. After he put the box he was

□

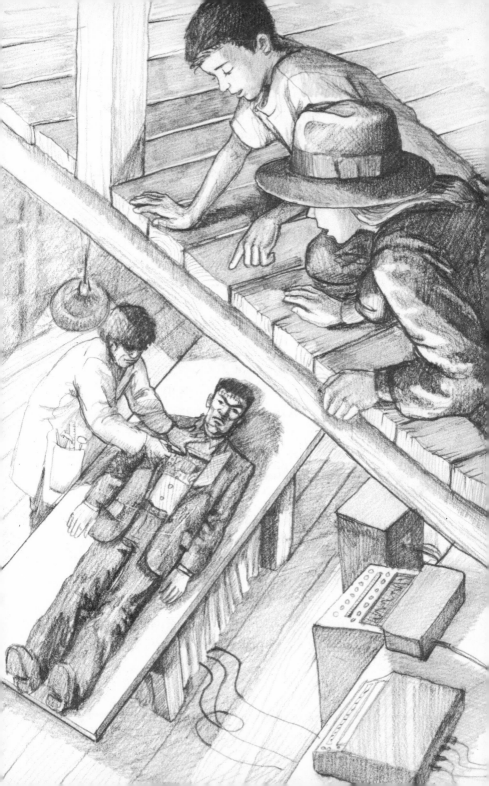

carrying on a worktable, I noticed words were printed on the front of his T-shirt. But because of the angle, I couldn't read what they said.

"Where have you been, Bruce?" the man in the lab coat demanded irritably. "I've been waiting for those parts."

"Sorry," the young man apologized. "It took the folks at the factory quite awhile to find everything you wanted."

"It's a wonder those company people get *anything* done," the older man snorted. "That's why *I* work alone."

The young man opened a locker and put on a lab coat. Then he joined the older man at the table, and together they began examining the wires inside the monster's chest. The older man began chuckling.

"There were some more kids sneaking around here last night," he said. "I used Frankie to scare them off. You should have seen them run."

"Great," Bruce laughed. "Now we know Frankie can do what he's supposed to do."

I glanced from the man over to the window, where I saw Frog peeking inside. I tapped Sarah's arm and pointed.

"I bet he's wondering what happened to us," Sarah whispered.

□

Suddenly Frog began knocking at the window. When the startled men looked over, he began making funny faces at them. Funny faces are easy for Frog.

"He's trying to draw them outside," Sarah said. "Get ready."

Frog's plan only half worked. With a cry of anger, the older man dropped his tools and hurried out of the barn. The younger man just shook his head and kept working on the robot.

"He's got his back to the door," Sarah pointed out. "Let's go. It's our only chance."

We crawled back to the ladder. Sarah started down first.

"Please don't look back," I thought as I followed her.

But no sooner did my sneakers hit the floor than Bruce glanced over his shoulder.

"Hey, you kids!" he yelled. "What are you doing in here?"

6

SARAH AND I RAN out the door and almost knocked the older man down as he tried to come back in. Now we could hear *him* shouting at us as we charged across the barnyard.

We never looked back and the men didn't chase us. As we turned from the driveway onto Misty Hollow Road, we saw Frog running up ahead. We called out to him and he waited for us to catch up.

"Boy, am I glad to see you guys," he panted. "I guess my plan to spring you worked."

□

"Good job, Fenniman!" Sarah declared, patting him on the back.

As we filled him in on what had happened to us, I kept an eye behind us, in case we were being followed. I felt safer when the fields disappeared and the road was again surrounded by thick woods.

"So what do you think is going on back there?" Frog asked.

"I'm not sure yet," Sarah admitted. "I bet the older man is the inventor who bought the farm. We know he's building a monster robot . . ."

"And he doesn't like people snooping around," I added.

"Who was the younger guy?" Frog wondered, as we left Misty Hollow Road and turned onto Route 19.

"I don't know," Sarah replied. "His name is Bruce and he brought the inventor some parts and was helping him."

"Watch it!" I cried.

Up ahead I saw four boys walking toward us down the highway. It was Franklin O'Grady and his gang! They hadn't spotted us yet, and we didn't want them to. I'd rather run into a nest of wasps than those four.

□

We dove for cover behind some nearby bushes. Peeking out, we saw the four leave the highway and disappear into the woods.

"Must be a trail there," Sarah said, after we were sure they were gone. "Come on."

We went to the spot where they had entered the woods. Sure enough, hidden in the brush was the entrance to a trail.

"Wonder where it goes," I said.

"Let's follow it and see," Sarah said enthusiastically.

"No way," I cried. "You'd have to be crazy to follow Franklin O'Grady and his gang into Misty Woods."

"Those guys have been spending a lot of time out here," Sarah persisted. "Don't you want to know what they're up to?"

"No," Frog answered. "I'm going home and work on Super-Duper Sleuths."

All the way back to town Sarah tried to change our minds, but it was no use. We finally split up and agreed to meet at the diner for dinner.

That night it seemed like every hungry person in western Pennsylvania wanted to eat at Lannigan's Miracle Diner. The place was jumping, and I loved it.

□

I spent most of the evening running the dishwasher. Later, Dad asked me to go out and help Goldie and Mabel clear tables. As I left the kitchen through the swinging doors, I ran into Frog and Sarah.

"I have to clear some tables," I told them, "and then we can eat."

"Grandpa is going to join us," Sarah said. "We'll wait for him by the cash register."

"Clark?" Mabel said, after I reported to her. "The guy in booth six just finished his dinner. Clear it for me and ask him if he wants dessert."

I grabbed a big tray and walked up the row of booths and counter stools.

"Can I interest you in some dessert?" I asked the man in booth six, as I began to load his dishes on the tray. "The chocolate cream pie is extra good tonight."

"Sounds great," the man answered. "And when you bring it, you can tell me what you were doing in Dr. Becker's barn today."

I dropped the plate I was holding with a clatter. For the first time I really looked at the customer in booth six. It was Bruce!

□

7

"AND TELL YOUR friends to join us," Bruce said, nodding over at Sarah and Frog, who were now staring.

"Yes, sir," I said, picking up the tray.

"He recognizes us," I told Sarah and Frog as I passed them on my way into the kitchen. "And he wants to talk."

"We're in for it now," Frog moaned. "He'll probably have us arrested for trespassing."

On my way back, I picked up a slice of pie from the pastry rack. When I got to the booth,

□

Sarah and Frog were already there, looking nervous.

"All right, kids," Bruce said as I slid into the booth. "Explain what you were doing, sneaking into Dr. Becker's barn."

Frog and I looked at Sarah. It was her fault we were in trouble. Let her do the talking.

"I'm a detective," Sarah replied calmly. "Clark and Frog are my associates."

"Not that we ever asked to be," Frog muttered under his breath.

"We heard reports that a crazy inventor was building a Frankenstein monster out at the old Harley farm," Sarah went on. "We were investigating those reports when you saw us."

While Sarah talked, I was relieved to see Bruce beginning to smile.

"Grady Becker is an inventor, and he may be eccentric," Bruce finally chuckled, "but he's not crazy."

"Then why is he building a robot monster?" Sarah demanded.

"Have you ever heard of Pennywood Park?" Bruce asked.

"Of course," Sarah answered. "That's the big amusement park in Pittsburgh."

"How about the Too Wonderful Toy Company?"

□

"They're in Pittsburgh, too," Frog said.

"Pennywood Park is building a new attraction called Haunted House Horrors," Bruce explained. "They've hired the Too Wonderful Toy Company to build them a mechanical Frankenstein to lurk inside and scare people."

That's when I noticed what the words on his T-shirt said. Too Wonderful Toys Are Just Too Wonderful!

"Do you and this Grady Becker work for the Too Wonderful Toy Company?" Sarah asked.

"*I* work for them," Bruce answered, "but not Dr. Becker. He's what's known as an *independent* toy inventor. The Too Wonderful people have hired him to build the Frankenstein robot for them. He's worked on special jobs like this for them before."

"The new owner of the Harley farm is a *toy* inventor?" Frog exclaimed.

Bruce nodded. "Grady Becker has invented some of the best-selling toys of all time. His specialty is electronic, battery-operated, and wind-up toys. Ever heard of Purring Puffy?"

"I had one of those when I was a kid!" Sarah cried. "It was a cute, fluffy kitten. When you patted its head, it purred real loud. I loved it!"

"Puffy was one of Grady Becker's ideas," Bruce said. "He sold the idea to the Majestic Toy

□

Company of Boston. I bet Majestic sold a million Purring Puffys."

"I'm sort of a toy inventor myself," Frog piped up. "I've just invented a new board game called . . ."

"How long will you be working with Dr. Becker?" Sarah interrupted.

"Until the Frankie project is completed," Bruce answered. "You might say Too Wonderful has me on loan to Dr. Becker."

Just then, Conrad Capshaw walked up to the booth. As usual, Sarah's grandfather looked very distinguished with his neatly combed silver hair and dark suit.

"Bruce Miller!" Mr. Capshaw exclaimed, shaking the young man's hand. "How are you?"

"Grandpa?" Sarah wondered. "You two know each other?"

"I'm one of the lawyers for the Too Wonderful Toy Company," Mr. Capshaw said. "How do you kids know Bruce?"

"We just sort of struck up a conversation," Bruce quickly replied.

Bruce and Mr. Capshaw talked business for a while and then Bruce said he had to get home to Pittsburgh. I walked to the cash register with him.

□

"Thanks for not telling on us," I said.

"Forget it," Bruce smiled. "When I was your age, I couldn't have resisted checking out a monster rumor either."

As I walked back to the booth, I was beaming. We hadn't gotten into trouble. And, best of all, the mystery of the Frankenstein monster was safely solved. I didn't know then that the *real* mystery was about to begin.

□

8

AFTER DINNER we went over to Frog's house and worked on Super-Duper Sleuths. Or rather, Sarah and Frog worked on that silly game. I watched television, with Churchill the bulldog sleeping next to me on the couch.

During a commercial I got up and looked out the window. It was getting dark and the street-lights were coming on. Suddenly, four boys came strutting down the street. When I recognized them, I automatically ducked back.

"What's the matter?" Sarah called from the

□

card table where they had the game spread out.

"Franklin O'Grady and his gang just went down the street," I said.

Sarah jumped up. "Let's tail them!"

Frog shook his head. "I'd rather follow Jack the Ripper."

"Those guys just might be on their way to Misty Woods. Maybe we can find out what they're up to."

Now that the case of the robot monster was solved, I knew Sarah was desperate for a mystery. Even if it was just following the O'Grady bunch around. Frog and I looked at each other and shrugged our shoulders. We knew there was no use saying "no."

Frog grabbed a flashlight and we stepped out into the night.

"Which way were they going?" Sarah asked.

I pointed down the street, and we headed in that direction. By the time we reached the corner and looked around, it was clear the gang had vanished.

"I bet they're going out to that secret trail," Sarah said. "Let's go that way."

But by the time we were on Route 19, there was still no sign of Franklin.

"I guess they weren't coming out here after

□

all," I said, hoping that meant we could go home. I should have known better.

"Since we've come this far, we might as well explore that trail anyway," Sarah replied cheerfully. "We might pick up some clues."

"Do you get the feeling we're being *had*," I muttered to Frog.

We found the thick brush that hid the entrance to the trail. Sarah took the flashlight from Frog and led the way. At first, it was an easy hike, with the path winding gently back and forth through the thick woods. But after awhile, it began to slope downwards, getting steeper as it led us into Misty Hollow.

The hollow is a narrow valley that runs through the middle of Misty Woods. As we hiked down, wisps of fog began to coil around our legs like ghostly snakes. As we neared the floor of the hollow, it got so thick we were enveloped in its damp embrace. The beam from the flashlight became a strange, floating ball.

"Now I see why this is called *Misty* Woods," Sarah whispered.

The sound of rushing water had been getting louder and louder. The trail finally leveled off again and stopped at the bank of a wide stream.

□

Sarah pointed the light across the water. The trail picked up again on the other side. There was only one way across.

"It's a swinging bridge," Sarah declared.

The bridge was made of boards attached to two ropes with two other ropes acting as handholds. All four ropes were tied to trees on both sides of the stream.

"Feels sturdy enough," Sarah said as she gave one of the ropes a shake. "Give it a try, Clark."

"Why me?" I cried.

"Because you're the heaviest. If it'll hold you, it'll hold Frog and me."

Grumbling to myself, I stepped up on the boards and gripped the handhold ropes. The boards creaked and the bridge swayed back and forth as I began to edge across. Below me, the stream had cut a deep path down the middle of the hollow. I was swinging above a spot where the water swirled in a dark pool.

After I reached the other side, Sarah and Frog crossed over. Then we picked up the trail and began to climb out of the hollow. The path eventually leveled off again and finally ended at a field. In the distance we could see the back of the barn and the house of the Harley farm.

"I bet Mr. Harley built that swinging bridge

□

back there," I said. "He must have used the trail as a shortcut."

We stared silently at the farm. Everything looked dark and still.

"Either Dr. Becker's not home or he's gone to bed," Frog said.

"Look!" Sarah hissed.

A dark figure had slipped around the corner of the barn and was creeping along the back wall. The man stopped under the only window on that side. At first, he tried to slide the window open. When that didn't work, he pulled something from his pocket and began prying at it.

"He's trying to break in!" Frog cried.

□

9

"Ssssshhhhhh!" Sarah and I tried to hush him.

It was too late. The figure spun away from the window and stood for a moment, staring out toward the edge of the woods where we were. Then he bolted around the corner of the barn.

"C'mon!" Sarah yelled.

We charged across the field and didn't stop until we reached the corner of the barn where the man had disappeared. Together, we peeked down the side. He was nowhere to be seen. Everything was as quiet and eerie as before.

□

"Be careful," Sarah whispered as she started down the side. "He may be waiting to ambush us at the other end."

By that time, I had come to my senses. Fear had replaced my excitement. Even if we found the man, what was Sarah planning to do? Pounce on him? We wouldn't stand a chance. There was no way I was going on with this manhunt. I knew Frog felt the same way.

Sarah stopped and looked back at us.

"Maybe you two better stay here and keep watch," she whispered. "If anything happens to me, you run and get help."

"Good idea," I sighed with relief.

"*Great* idea," Frog added.

We held our breath as Sarah edged her way along the side of the barn. When she reached the front corner, she looked all around. Then she shrugged her shoulders and signaled us to join her.

"He's gone," she whispered.

"It's like he vanished into thin air," I said.

"Maybe it was a ghost?" Frog suggested.

"A ghost wouldn't need to pry a window open to get in," Sarah snapped.

"Maybe it was Dr. Becker?" I added.

"Why would he need to break into his own

barn? Besides, I don't think he's even home. His car isn't here."

"Well, whoever it was is gone now," Frog said. "And we should be too."

We crossed back through the field and stopped at the edge of the woods to look back. The farm still looked dark and deserted.

"We'll come back tomorrow and tell Dr. Becker what we saw," Sarah declared.

"Are you crazy?" I cried. "He'll think we did it!"

"It's our duty," Sarah said solemnly.

We hiked the trail back down to the swinging bridge. This time we crossed together, with Sarah leading the way and me bringing up the rear with the flashlight.

Halfway across, something made me glance nervously over my shoulder. I gasped when I realized someone was standing on the bank we had just left. I quickly aimed the flashlight and for a split second, the beam held a man's face like a deer in the headlights of a car.

"Point the light *this* way, Clark," Frog complained. "I can't see where I'm stepping."

"Lannigan?" Sarah called out. "What's the matter?"

"Someone's watching us back there," I cried.

□

I looked again. Rocks, bushes, trees, and the end of the bridge seemed to be drifting in the ghostly fog. But that was all.

"I don't see anything," Sarah said.

"I don't either," I admitted. "Now."

I shook my head. I was beginning to wonder if Frog was right. Maybe we were dealing with a ghost!

10

"ARE YOU *sure* he was Asian?" Sarah asked me for the hundredth time.

It was the next day and we were sitting in a booth in the diner having lunch.

"I'm *pretty* sure," I answered for the hundredth time. "I only saw him for a split second before he disappeared."

"Like a ghost," Frog added.

After crossing the bridge the night before, I had told them that I thought the man I had seen on the other side was Asian or of Asian descent.

□

"Did you recognize him?" Sarah had asked.

"Never saw him before," I answered.

"I wonder what he was doing in Misty Woods at that hour?" Sarah now said, after taking a bite of her chicken salad sandwich. "Was he the same man we saw trying to break into the barn?"

Just then, there was a banging on the window next to the booth.

"Look," Frog pointed. "It's the first runner-up in the Wilsonburg Ugly Pageant."

Franklin O'Grady was standing outside, pressing his huge face against the glass. He looked like a cooked ham with squinty eyes.

"If you guys know what's good for you, you'll stay out of Misty Woods," Franklin yelled through the glass.

Then he shook his fist at us and stomped off.

"It's time for us to go out and tell Dr. Becker what we saw last night," Sarah declared, straightening her hat.

"By the way," I said to Frog as we left the diner. "If Franklin O'Grady is the first runner-up in the Wilsonburg Ugly Pageant, who's the winner?"

"My dog, Churchill," Frog answered with a grin.

We laughed all the way out of town. When we

□

got to the farm we saw Dr. Becker's car parked in the barnyard. The barn door was open a crack, so we peeked in. The toy inventor was inside working on Frankie.

"Dr. Becker?" Sarah called. "May we talk to you a minute?"

At first, he looked startled. Then mad. Dropping his tools on the monster's chest, he stepped toward us.

"What do you kids want?" he demanded. "You're trespassing, you know."

Then he got a look at Frog.

"You're the one who made faces at me yesterday!"

"Dr. Becker?" Sarah spoke up quickly. "We believe that someone tried to break into your barn last night."

"What?" the inventor cried in surprise.

"It happened at the back window," Sarah said, as we led him to the rear of the barn.

"You're right!" he exclaimed, after examining the window. "Someone has tried to pry this open."

"We didn't get a good look at him," Sarah explained. "But we did scare him off."

Dr. Becker looked at us suspiciously. "What were you kids doing out here at night anyway?"

□

Becker stared closely at each of us. Then his face softened, and I could tell he believed our story.

"Thank you for coming out here to tell me," he said gruffly. "*And* for scaring the intruder away."

"Do you think he wanted to steal Frankie?" Frog asked.

The inventor shook his head. "This window doesn't lead to the workshop where the robot is. It leads to my office at the back of the barn."

I remembered when Sarah and I had tried to escape from the barn. We had run to a door at the back, only to find it locked. It must lead into the office.

"Do you keep money in your office?" Sarah asked.

"No, something *much* more valuable. I keep top secret plans and ideas for future toys in my office. A lot of toy companies would love to get their hands on those."

"Dr. Becker?" Frog stepped forward. "*I've* just invented a toy. It's a game called Super-Duper Sleuths. Would you like to see it sometime?"

I really expected Dr. Becker to say "no." For a moment, he seemed lost in thought. Then, much to my surprise, he actually gave Frog a little smile.

□

"Of course," he replied. "Bring it out sometime after dinner and I'll look at it."

Just then a mini-van pulled into the barnyard.

"Here's Bruce," Dr. Becker said. "You'll have to go now."

With that, he walked away and we did the same. After we crossed the field, Sarah paused to write in the little notebook she always carries in her back pocket. Frog and I looked at each other. We both knew what the notebook meant.

"Well, men," Sarah beamed. "It looks like we're on another case!"

□

11

"Aren't you jumping the gun a little?" I said, as we walked back to town.

"You heard what Dr. Becker said," Sarah replied. "He keeps top secret toy ideas and plans locked in his office. And of all the windows in the barn, the intruder chose the *office* window to try and break into."

"There may be another reason for that," Frog pointed out. "Maybe it was just a regular burglar looking for stuff to steal. He picked the back window because it's farthest from the house."

Sarah just shook her head. I could see there

□

was no use trying to talk her out of her mystery.

The afternoon was hot, so we stopped at the diner for cold drinks. We sat at the counter and watched Fred McGhee, the grillman, pour ice cold root beers into frosted mugs.

"Why didn't you tell Dr. Becker about the Asian man I saw in the woods last night?" I asked Sarah.

"A good detective doesn't tell everything she knows," she replied smugly.

"I bet that guy didn't have anything to do with the break-in anyway," Frog added.

Just then my little sister walked by with Mr. Vroom Vroom.

"Clara?" Sarah asked. "Can I see your truck for a minute?"

We watched as Sarah turned the truck over and squinted at the tiny words stamped on the bottom.

"Made in Taiwan!" she declared triumphantly. "A lot of toys are made over there. And just where is Taiwan?"

"I know! I know!" Frog cried, waving his hand in the air. "Pick me! Pick me!"

"This isn't school, Frog," Sarah growled. "Just answer the question."

"Taiwan is an island off the coast of mainland China," he answered proudly.

□

"Very good," Sarah replied, handing the truck back to Clara. "And what did Clark notice about the man standing near the swinging bridge the other night?"

"I know! I know!" Frog exclaimed, waving his hand again.

Sarah groaned and buried her face in her hands.

Frog grinned. "Clark said the man looked Asian."

"I know what you're getting at," I said.

"Good, because I don't," Frog admitted.

"You think a spy from a toy company in Taiwan is trying to steal Dr. Becker's toy ideas."

"Exactly!" Sarah said excitedly. "And tonight we're going to stake out the farm and try to prove my theory."

"I hate stakeouts," I grumbled.

It was dark in Misty Woods and we were crouched in bushes at the edge of the field, watching the back of the barn. Yellow light poured out of its windows into the night.

"Yeah," Frog piped up. "The only steak out I want is at the diner and it's medium rare."

"Besides," I added. "No one is going to try and break into the barn while Dr. Becker is in there working."

□

"Stop complaining," Sarah hissed. "Let's spread out. If you see anything, make a sound like an owl."

I sure didn't like the idea of splitting up. Even though the moon had turned the field into a silvery sea, the woods were black and plenty spooky. Before I could protest, Sarah slipped away and vanished into the thick brush.

I left Frog crouching where he was and made my way farther down the edge of the woods. I kept going until I came to a tiny clearing. It looked like a good place to settle into. From there I had a great view of both the back and side of the barn, as well as part of the house. Too bad someone else had the same idea!

I didn't see the man until it was too late and he had seen me, too. With a gasp, he jumped to his feet.

"Whooo!" I squeaked.

I sounded like a very small owl that has just swallowed a very large mouse. I was too scared to even run. Without knowing what I was doing, I flicked on my flashlight. Standing in the trembling beam of light was the Asian man!

I stared helplessly as the look on his face went from quite startled to very angry. With a growl, he moved toward me!

□

12

"Whooooooooo!" I shrieked.

It was the mother of all hoots. I sounded like a five hundred-pound owl with a terrible beak-ache. The hoot seemed to push the panic from my brain down to my feet. I turned and bolted.

"Whooooo!" I screeched, as I plunged blindly through the woods. "Whooo-ahhhhh!"

My hoot turned into a cry when I tripped over a root and went sprawling. With the wind knocked out of me, I could only lie there watching the dark figure stomping toward me.

"Clark!" I heard Frog cry. "Clark!"

□

Suddenly Frog popped out of the brush and planted himself between me and the advancing figure.

"Stay back!" my best friend warned. "I know karate!"

The only thing Frog knows about karate is what he sees on television. He was standing his ground, waving his arms in the air like a crazed penguin.

"Clark? Frog?" Sarah cried, as she joined the strange scene.

She turned on her flashlight and I gasped with relief. The man walking up to us wasn't Asian. It was Bruce Miller.

"What's going on here?" he demanded angrily.

"The Asian man," I said, as Frog helped me to my feet. "He was over there. I saw him."

"What are you talking about?" Bruce snapped, turning on his own flashlight and scanning the woods. "What Asian man?"

Before I could open my mouth, we heard a voice yelling from the direction of the barn.

"Who's out there?" the voice called. "What's going on?"

"It's Becker!" Bruce hissed. "Turn off your lights and come with me. If he catches you here, you're in big trouble."

Bruce led us through the woods and down

□

into the hollow beside the swinging bridge. Once he felt we were safe, he demanded an explanation. Sarah gave him an honest one.

"Dr. Becker told me what you saw out here last night," Bruce said when she was finished. "But he didn't say anything about an Asian man."

"That's because we didn't tell him that part," Sarah admitted.

"Where did you come from?" I asked.

"Dr. Becker and I are working late tonight on Frankie," Bruce explained. "Becker thought he heard voices coming from the woods. He sent me to investigate."

"What do *you* think is going on?" I asked.

"Do you really want to know what I think?" Bruce said, with an angry edge to his voice. "I think that last night some country burglar figured he'd break into the barn and steal a chain saw or something. Now Becker is all paranoid that some toy company is trying to steal his ideas. He's even talking about putting bars on the windows and getting a guard dog."

"He's paranoid?" Sarah wondered.

"That's right. A long time ago some company stole one of his toy ideas and made a million dollars off of it. Ever since then, he thinks everyone is out to steal his ideas and cash in on them."

☐

"But what about the Asian man?" I asked. "Do you think he's the country burglar you were talking about?"

"Of course not!" Bruce answered. "He's probably just some innocent guy who likes evening walks in the woods and keeps running into you kids."

Feeling foolish, I stared down at my sneakers.

"Look," Bruce said in a softer voice. "You kids are clever. But you're all wrong about this. Now go home, so I can get back to work."

Bruce waited on the bank while we crossed the bridge. Even as we hiked up the other side of the hollow, I could see the beam from his flashlight down beside the stream. I guess he wanted to make sure we were really going.

"Well," Frog said as we left the woods behind. "I guess we were wrong about that mystery."

"Who are you going to believe?" Sarah asked angrily. "Bruce or me?"

And before we could answer "Bruce" she stomped off.

□

13

WHEN I GOT TO the diner the next morning I found Sarah and Frog waiting for me.

"Mr. Capshaw is taking us to visit the Too Wonderful Toy Company!" Frog said excitedly. "It was Sarah's idea!"

"I heard Grandpa say he had a meeting with Jack Herbert, the president of the company," Sarah explained. "I asked him if we could go along. We're going to get a special tour. Maybe we'll learn something to help us with our case."

□

Mom and Dad said I could go, and Mr. Capshaw picked us up out front.

It only took us thirty minutes to drive down along the Monongahela River to Pittsburgh. The Too Wonderful Toy Company is right on the river. There are several large factory buildings near the water and railroad tracks.

After parking the car, Mr. Capshaw led us to a modern brick building closer to the road. We stepped into a cool air-conditioned reception area.

We stopped at a security station where a guard checked an appointment book and gave us visitor badges to wear. She then checked inside Mr. Capshaw's briefcase.

"What's she looking for?" Sarah asked.

"She wants to make sure I'm not sneaking a camera inside," Mr. Capshaw answered. "Toy companies, like Too Wonderful, have to be careful that none of their ideas or plans slip out."

The guard held a door open for us, and we stepped into a long hall. A young man came out of an office and greeted Mr. Capshaw. He was dressed casually in slacks and a Too Wonderful T-shirt.

"This is Jerry Nevins," Mr. Capshaw introduced us. "He's an assistant vice president here."

□

"But right now I'm a tour guide," Jerry Nevins said, with a grin. "Mr. Herbert asked me to show you kids around while he meets with Conrad."

Mr. Capshaw headed for the elevators, and Mr. Nevins led us out behind the building. We climbed into a golf cart and he drove us down toward the factory buildings.

"Too Wonderful is involved in all kinds of toys for all ages," Mr. Nevins explained as we bounced along. "We hire other companies to make our parts for us. The parts come in by truck and railroad. Then our workers assemble and package the toys here and we ship the finished product out."

Mr. Nevins drove the golf cart into the first factory building. Workers stood on long assembly lines running machines and putting together neat-looking toys. Mr. Nevins stopped the cart at the end of one line, and led us over to the conveyor belt.

"This is Mathmo the Robot," he said, picking up one of the twelve-inch metal robots. "Not only does he walk and talk, but there's a calculator built inside to help kids with math."

"He's neat!" Frog exclaimed.

"We're expecting him to be a big seller," Mr. Nevins replied as we followed him to another

□

conveyor belt where beautiful dolls were rolling along.

"Very soon you'll be seeing commercials on television for this doll. She's called Princess Carmella, and she'll come with her very own unicorn to ride."

"I'd like a unicorn to ride," Frog commented.

After touring the packing factory and warehouse, Mr. Nevins took us back to the administration building and showed us around. One wing was devoted to publicity and promotion. Another wing housed the safety department where the toys were tested.

"This is the heart of the company," Mr. Nevins pointed out as we stepped off the elevator on the third floor. "The creative department. This is where our inventors and engineers come up with the wonderful toy ideas that make everything else possible."

On this floor there were offices, conference rooms, labs, and workshops. We walked by a large glass window that looked into a conference room. Inside, a group of men and women were sitting around a long table. A man I recognized was standing before them pointing to drawings clipped to an easel.

"It's Dr. Becker," I pointed out.

□

"You know him?" Mr. Nevins said. "He's in there, pitching one of his ideas to our creative officers."

"Pitching ideas?" Sarah wondered.

"Most of our new toy ideas come from our own staff," Mr. Nevins explained. "But sometimes we *do* buy ideas from independent inventors like Grady Becker. As a matter of fact, Mathmo the Robot was his invention."

Farther down the hall, we saw Bruce Miller at work in a lab. We waved, but he didn't see us. At the end of our tour, Mr. Nevins treated us in the cafeteria. While we snacked, Frog told him all about Super-Duper Sleuths. Mr. Nevins tried to look interested, but he didn't invite Frog to bring his game in to "pitch" it to the Too Wonderful creative officers.

Mr. Capshaw met us and we thanked Mr. Nevins for his time. Back at the reception area, we turned in our badges and waited while the guard checked Mr. Capshaw's briefcase again.

"Boy!" Frog declared as we drove away. "Security is sure tight there."

"It has to be," Mr. Capshaw replied. "Toys are big business. Millions of dollars can be made and *lost* on a single toy. Other companies would love to know what Too Wonderful is going to do next."

□

Suddenly Sarah leaned over toward my ear.

"Now tell me," she whispered. "Do you *really* believe the intruder at Dr. Becker's was trying to steal a chain saw like Bruce said?"

My answer surprised me.

"No."

14

OUR TOY COMPANY tour had gotten Frog all
excited about showing Dr. Becker *his* game.
After dinner that evening we headed out to the
farm.

"So you think Bruce is wrong about the intruder just being a regular burglar?" Frog asked
as he shifted his game box from one arm to the
other.

"I don't think Bruce even believes that story
himself," Sarah snapped.

"But that's what he told us."

□

66

"Bruce told us a number of things last night that I don't think were true."

"Like what?"

"I don't think Bruce was working late with Dr. Becker last night the way he said," Sarah answered. "He told us Dr. Becker heard our voices and sent him to investigate. But we never talked above a whisper. He couldn't have heard us."

"But Dr. Becker *did* hear Clark when he started to yell," Frog pointed out.

"Bruce was *already* in the woods by then," Sarah replied. "And the only way to get to the woods from the barn is across the field. Did you see anyone cross that field? I sure didn't."

"You're saying Bruce was in the woods all along," I said. "What was he doing?"

"I think Bruce believes that a rival company *did* try to break into Dr. Becker's office looking for his ideas and plans."

"Why does he care?" I wondered. "Dr. Becker doesn't work for Too Wonderful. He's an independent."

"But he *does* sell ideas to Too Wonderful," Sarah reasoned. "I don't think Too Wonderful wants a rival toy company stealing Dr. Becker's ideas and cashing in on them *before* they have a chance to buy them if they want them."

□

"You're saying that Bruce was in the woods conducting his own *secret* investigation for Too Wonderful," Frog remarked.

"Exactly," Sarah nodded her head. "That's why he hurried us away when Dr. Becker started shouting from the barn. He didn't want Dr. Becker to see us *or* him."

"And he doesn't want us involved because we might mess up his investigation," I finished.

By then we had hiked down into Misty Hollow and started across the swinging bridge. Halfway over, Sarah froze. I looked over her shoulder and saw Franklin O'Grady standing on the other side with a big smirk on his face. One of his buddies was slouching next to him.

"I thought I told you to stay out of Misty Woods," Franklin snarled.

"You *thought*?" Sarah cried in amazement. "I didn't know you knew *how* to think, O'Grady!"

Suddenly I heard snickering coming from the other bank. I glanced over my shoulder and saw Franklin's other two buddies standing beside the bridge behind us. We were trapped!

"This is no time to make him mad," I warned Sarah as I felt the bridge swaying under our feet.

"Sure is hot," Franklin laughed evilly. "How about a swim?"

□

He and his buddy began to push and shake the bridge. The two on the bank behind us did the same. In a few seconds the bridge was swaying wildly back and forth.

"Look, guys!" I heard Franklin hoot. "Three swingers!"

Frog was the first to go. With his toy box in one hand, he only had one hand left to grip the rope. With a shriek, he went flying headfirst over the rail.

Sarah went next. She could have lasted longer, but she tried to edge her way across to get at Franklin. Her feet shot out from under her and she skidded off.

I hung on alone. It was like being on a crazy ride at Pennywood Amusement Park. Back and forth, back and forth, the bridge swung wider and wider until I felt sick. I knew Franklin and his gang could go on swinging the bridge a lot longer than I could hold on. Finally I just gave up and jumped.

I plunged six feet into the swirling pool. The cold water closed over me with a whoosh before I shot to the surface sputtering and shivering. The pool was only about four feet deep, so I was able to stand up and wade toward Frog.

"My game!" he was yelling as he lunged at floating pieces of paper. "My game!"

□

Like blossoms at the end of spring, the paper was rushing away in the current. As the box itself sailed out of sight downstream, I put my arm around his trembling shoulders.

"It's gone!" he wailed. "Just like my ants!"

□

15

Frog's game was gone and so were the creeps who had dunked us. By the time Sarah waded to shore, Franklin and his gang had disappeared into the woods. All we could hear were their hoots and hollers somewhere in the distance.

There was nothing we could do but go home. As we sloshed and dripped our way back to town, Sarah and I tried to cheer up Frog. It was no use.

"Super-Duper Sleuths is Super-Soggy Sleuths now," he moaned.

□

The next morning, as I was finishing my shift at the diner, Frog came into the kitchen.

"Sarah's down at the library," he said. "She wants us to meet her there."

The Wilsonburg Public Library is my second favorite place in town. The diner is the first, of course. We stepped into the cool bustle of the library and headed for the reference desk.

"Hi, guys!" Mr. Mehlin, the librarian, greeted us. "What can I do for you this morning?"

"We're looking for Sarah Capshaw," I explained.

"Conrad Capshaw's granddaughter? She's using one of the microfilm machines in the Periodical Room."

We thanked him and headed for the big room where all the magazines were kept. We found Sarah sitting at a microfilm machine turning a knob which made the film fly from one reel to the other. The table around the machine was piled with thick books and paper filled with notes.

"What are you doing?" I asked as Frog and I sat down beside her.

"Research," she answered. "The library has old newspapers on microfilm. These books are indexes. I can look up different subjects in the indexes and they tell me which issue of the paper

□

has the story I want. Then I just put the right reel of film in the machine and run it through until I come to the right issue."

"And what have you found out?" I asked.

"There have been a number of articles about Dr. Becker. I found out that he used to work for the Majestic Toy Company of Boston before he quit to work independently."

"Did the article say why he quit?" I wondered.

"Dr. Becker told the reporter he was unhappy with Majestic because they were getting more and more into war toys."

"War toys?"

"You know, toy tanks, missiles, soldiers, stuff like that. Dr. Becker said he was tired of being forced to invent miniature toys of destruction. He especially hates toy guns."

We watched as Sarah turned the knob on the machine again. Magnified pages of the paper flew across the screen in a blur. She slowed the reel down as the page she wanted came up.

"Will you look at that?" she whistled.

The headline at the top of the business section said HORJING CORP. BUYS MAJESTIC. We leaned closer to the screen and read the article, which was a year old. It said that the Majestic Toy Company of Boston had just been bought by the

□

Horjing Corporation, one of the world's leading toy manufacturers, based in Taiwan.

"Do you think there's any connection between this Horjing Corporation and the Asian man trying to break into Dr. Becker's office?"

"I sure do," Sarah replied grimly.

"Shouldn't we warn Dr. Becker?" Frog asked. "Or Bruce?"

"Of course not!" Sarah snapped as she rewound the film. "They won't believe us. All we have are theories. No real proof. And Bruce has already told us to get lost. The best way for us to help is to get the proof we need to solve this case."

"What next?" I asked.

"I want to go back to the farm and talk with Dr. Becker," Sarah said, putting the film and indexes away. "We need to try and find out more about what's in his office. Is it *really* worth a company committing a crime to see what's in there?"

"How can we go back?" Frog wondered. "I don't have my game to show him anymore and he doesn't like company."

"But you still *do* have the game," I insisted, tapping Frog's forehead with my finger. "It's up here!"

□

"Clark's right," Sarah agreed. "Even if you can't *show* it to him, you can still *tell* him about it."

"Yeah," Frog exclaimed. "This may be my only chance to get some tips from a real toy inventor."

"Frog, my friend," Sarah declared, patting him on the back. "You just may be our ticket into the heart of this mystery—Dr. Grady Becker."

"Did you hear that, Clark?" Frog beamed. "I'm a ticket!"

□

16

WE DECIDED TO visit the farm that evening after dinner. Our best chance of talking to Dr. Becker would come if we didn't interrupt his work.

Fortified by a supper of chicken pot pie at the diner, we traveled the now familiar route to the swinging bridge. But before we could cross the stream, Sarah held up a warning hand. Frog and I froze and listened. Above the sound of rushing water we could hear voices drifting into the hollow.

"Hide!" Sarah warned.

□

Frog and I followed her into some thick bushes clustered near the bridge. A few minutes later Franklin led his gang down the path past the bushes where we crouched. They stopped at the bridge and began laughing hysterically.

"Did you see Capshaw hit the water yesterday?" Franklin hooted. "She looked like a walrus doing a belly flop."

I glanced nervously over at Sarah. Her body had gone stiff with anger. I knew she was about to blow.

"Revenge!" she hissed. "Get ready to run."

"Oh, no!" Frog whimpered as Sarah walked around the bush and straight up to Franklin.

"What are you doing here?" Franklin demanded.

"I'm ant watching," Sarah declared cheerfully.

"What's that?"

"It's like bird watching," she explained. "But instead of looking up, you look down."

Sarah squatted down near Franklin's feet and pointed at the ground near his sneakers.

"Ah-ha!" she cried excitedly. "It's the rare Pinchme Terriblus ant."

"Pinchme what?" Franklin said, looking completely bewildered.

Suddenly Sarah reached out and pinched his leg.

□

"Ouch!" Franklin yelled, jumping back. But he didn't leap far enough to stop Sarah from pinching his other leg.

"Ow!" he shrieked, jumping back again.

"Watch out, Franklin," Sarah yelled as she crawled toward him. "He's going up your pants leg!"

"You're crazy!" Franklin hollered, jumping from one foot to the other. "Get away from me!"

Franklin kept hopping back and Sarah kept lunging at his legs until they reached the edge of the stream. Then Sarah jumped to her feet, put both hands on Franklin's chest and pushed. With a final howl, Franklin tumbled backward into the water.

For several seconds everyone but Franklin was frozen in place. While he splashed and sputtered like a water buffalo, his three buddies just stared as if they couldn't believe what had happened to their leader.

And then everything quickly unfroze. Franklin began to climb out of the water and his buddies lunged at Sarah, who bolted for the path. Frog and I were right behind her.

The O'Grady gang may be big and strong, but they're also slow. By the time the path leveled off out of the hollow, we had left them far behind.

□

We didn't stop running until we were back at the highway where we started.

"Sorry, guys," Sarah apologized after we caught our breath. "If I hadn't lost my head, we could have tailed Franklin and maybe found out what he's up to out here."

"Forget it," I laughed. "It was worth getting even with him."

To avoid running into the gang again, we went to the farm by way of Misty Hollow Road. We found Dr. Becker sitting on his back porch smoking his pipe. When he saw us, he frowned as if we were interrupting his peace and quiet. Which we were.

"Dr. Becker?" Frog began nervously. "I'm the kid who invented a board game. You said I could show it to you."

The stern look on Dr. Becker's face softened, just like it had the last time Frog mentioned his game. There seemed to be something about it that touched the inventor.

"Where is this game?" Becker asked. "In your pocket?"

Before Frog could answer, Sarah looked across the yard at the barn.

"You got the bars put on the windows," she pointed out.

□

"They sure look strong," I added.

"Every window is now protected," the inventor replied. "And tomorrow, when I get my guard dog, no one will dare try to break in."

Sarah saw her opening.

"You must have some really valuable things in your office," she said.

"Valuable?" Dr. Becker snorted. "Young lady, locked in my office at this very moment are plans for the greatest toy idea of my career. When I'm finished developing it, it just may become the best-selling toy of all time. Toy companies will fight each other for the rights to it. It'll be a real bidding war!"

I shot a look at Sarah. She looked really excited.

"This is *big*, Lannigan," she whispered in my ear. "Bigger than I thought!"

□

17

"So TELL ME about this board game of yours,"
Dr. Becker said.

Frog shrugged his shoulders and told the
inventor about the watery end of Super-Duper
Sleuths. Dr. Becker shook his head sympatheti-
cally.

"You know, I invented a board game when I
was about your age," he remarked.

"Really?"

"I grew up on an isolated farm in New En-
gland," the inventor explained. "There wasn't

□

another child for miles around for me to play with. All I had for company were my books and imagination." Dr. Becker paused to relight his pipe.

"My parents didn't have much money," he went on. "But my father was good with his hands. I would think up toys and he would try and make them for me. It was great fun."

"Tell me about *your* game," Frog said.

"I called it Knights & Dragons. Dad carved the board and pieces out of wood. We spent many a cold winter's night playing that game by the fire. I usually won because I made up the rules!"

Dr. Becker stood up and tapped his pipe out on the porch rail.

"Maybe you'd like to see my collection."

He led us into the house and down the hall to a large room on the right. The room was filled with toys of all kinds. There were dolls, boats, robots, trucks, trains, and much more. Smaller toys were displayed on shelves which lined the walls. The larger toys were arranged on the floor.

"I got my Ph.D. in electronics," Dr. Becker explained. "That's why my specialty is wind-up, battery-operated, and electronic toys."

He showed us a clock decorated with little elves hanging on the hands.

□

"This is the Wee Watch. I designed it to help children learn to tell time."

He turned the hands until they pointed at twelve. Suddenly a tiny elflike voice spoke from inside the clock.

"The elves are on twelve. It's twelve o'clock."

"Look," Frog pointed at a robot on the shelf. "It's Mathmo."

"How do you know about Mathmo?" Dr. Becker wondered. "He hasn't even hit the market yet."

"We saw him during our tour of the Too Wonderful Toy Company," Sarah explained. "We also saw you in a meeting."

The inventor looked very pleased with himself.

"I was trying to sell Too Wonderful my idea for Beatrice the Butterfly. When you turn on her battery she spreads her beautiful rainbow wings back and forth. They bought it!"

Then he led us to a shelf near the door.

"These are my toy inventions that failed," he said, lifting down a cute doll and handing her to me. "This is Burping Belinda, my first doll when I worked for the Majestic Toy Company. Burp her."

I gently patted the doll's back and waited to hear a soft burp. What came out was a loud belch

□

that sounded like Big Walt after he eats a bowl of chili at the diner.

"I was never able to work out Belinda's bugs," the inventor said as he replaced the doll, "and needless to say Majestic chose not to market her."

"Why do you keep your failures?" Frog asked.

"Because I've learned something valuable from each and every failure. Something that helped make my next toy better. A good inventor is one who never gives up and uses failures to make successes."

Frog's eyes lit up. "I see what you mean. There were a lot of things I didn't like about my game. Things I wanted to change and make better. Now that I have to start over I can make a new, improved Super-Duper Sleuths!"

Dr. Becker was actually smiling as he lifted down another toy from the failure shelf. It was a little clown with a parachute attached to its back.

"This was Flummer the Flying Clown," he said sadly. "When you toss him high in the air, the chute opens and he drifts back to earth. I invented him while I was with Majestic. Somehow a rival toy company stole my idea. Before Majestic could release Flummer, this rival company hit the market with a toy penguin that worked the same way."

☐

"A knockoff," Frog said.

"What do you know about knockoffs?" Dr. Becker asked in surprise.

"I did some reading about the toy industry while I was working on my game," Frog answered. "When one company has a good toy idea, another company sometimes tries to cash in on the idea by coming out with another toy like it. It's called a knockoff."

"If you want to invent toys for a living," Dr. Becker warned him, "you'd better keep your ideas a secret for as long as you can."

Just then I glanced over at the window and saw a face pressed against the glass.

"What's the matter?" Sarah asked when I jumped.

"The Asian man!" I cried. "He's looking in at us!"

□

18

BY THE TIME the others looked, the face had disappeared. I was beginning to wonder if I was losing my mind. I seemed to be the only one who ever saw the Asian man. Dr. Becker walked over to the window and looked out.

"There's no one out there," he declared. "The sun must have been playing tricks with your eyes as it sets."

I opened my mouth to protest, but Sarah shot me a look that said, "Keep quiet."

"You kids will have to go now," Dr. Becker

□

said as he herded us into the hall and out to the back porch. "I have work to do."

We thanked him for visiting with us and walked down the steps. As we crossed the field toward the woods, I looked over my shoulder. Dr. Becker was still standing on the back porch staring at us.

"The Asian man *was* outside the window," I insisted.

"I believe you," Sarah agreed. "Something strange is going on back there."

"What do you mean?" Frog asked.

"Dr. Becker is paranoid about someone stealing his toy ideas," Sarah pointed out. "But he didn't seem the least bit worried that someone even *might* have been peeking in his window."

After we entered the cover of the woods, Sarah motioned us to be quiet. We followed her to some bushes where we had a good view of the back porch. Dr. Becker was still standing there staring at the spot where we had disappeared into the woods.

"He wants to make sure we're gone," Sarah whispered.

She was right, because a minute later another man stepped out from behind a tree and joined Dr. Becker on the porch. Though the sun had

□

set, there was still enough light for us to recognize the newcomer. It was the Asian man!

We stared in amazement as the two men shook hands. Then they stepped off the porch and walked toward the front doors of the barn, out of our sight.

"What the heck is going on?" Frog whispered.

I glanced over at Sarah. She looked just as puzzled as I felt.

"Let's sneak back to the barn," she finally suggested. "Maybe we can hear what they're saying."

"Let's just *stay put*." A voice nearby made us jump.

We looked up and found Bruce Miller standing over us. A pair of binoculars was hanging around his neck and he looked plenty mad.

"I thought I told you kids to stop snooping around out here," he growled.

"You said a lot of things," Sarah replied coolly. "And not all of it was the truth."

She then told him that we didn't think he was working late with Dr. Becker the night he caught us in the woods.

"I think you're working undercover for Too Wonderful," Sarah went on. "You know Dr. Becker is developing a top secret toy idea that's

☐

going to be worth millions. Too Wonderful is afraid another company will steal the idea from him before they can bid on it."

"You have some imagination," Bruce snickered.

"My grandfather, Conrad Capshaw, won't think this is so funny when I tell him," Sarah snapped back.

Bruce stopped laughing and moved to block her path.

"All right," he said, holding up his hands. "I admit you're right about me working undercover for Too Wonderful. But you're wrong about Becker. He's not the victim here. He's the villain."

"What?" Sarah cried.

"That's right," Bruce nodded grimly. "When it comes to stealing toy ideas, it's Grady Becker who's the thief."

□

19

Bruce glanced nervously toward the barn.

"Let's talk by the bridge," he said. "Becker might hear us if we stay here."

Dusk turned quickly to night as we walked down into the dark hollow. At the end of the swinging bridge we gathered around Bruce.

"Now tell me what you *think* is going on," he said. "I want to know everything you've seen and heard."

Sarah did just that. She started at the beginning and ended with our seeing Dr. Becker and the

□

Asian man shaking hands and heading toward the barn.

"Now it's your turn," she finished.

Bruce took a deep breath.

"For some time now, Mr. Herbert, the president of Too Wonderful, has suspected that someone is leaking company plans and ideas to our chief competitor . . ."

"The Majestic Toy Company of Boston," Sarah finished for him.

"That's right. And we believe that Grady Becker is the source of the leaks."

"But he doesn't even work for Too Wonderful," Frog protested. "He's an *independent* inventor."

"Yes," Bruce agreed, "but he is allowed into our research offices when he demonstrates his new toy ideas. He sees things there and our staff tells him things because they trust him."

"And he's working on Too Wonderful's Frankenstein project," Sarah pointed out.

"Which gives him even more chances to visit our offices where future projects are being planned," Bruce replied.

"And to *spy*," Sarah added.

"The problem is that we're having trouble proving any of this. That's where I come in. My

□

job is to help Becker with the Frankenstein project, but at the same time I'm also spying on *him*."

"That's why you've been hiding in the woods," I said.

"I've been secretly watching the farm, hoping to spot Becker meeting with his contact from Majestic."

"The Asian man is his contact," Sarah declared. "About a year ago the Horjing Corporation of Taiwan bought the Majestic Toy Company."

"Wow!" Bruce said admiringly. "You *are* good!"

I was glad I couldn't see Sarah's face in the dark. I figured she was looking pretty smug about then.

"I don't believe any of this!" Frog suddenly piped up. "Dr. Becker has invented some of the best-selling toys of all time. Why would he have to steal other people's ideas?"

"Yeah," I agreed. "We read that Dr. Becker *quit* working for Majestic because they were getting more and more into war toys. Why would he want to steal ideas for them now?"

"Blackmail," Bruce answered grimly. "I found out that Grady Becker didn't quit his job at Majestic. He was *fired*. I believe that Majestic found something out about him. Something bad."

□

"And now Majestic is blackmailing him," Sarah said, snapping her fingers. "They're *making* him spy on Too Wonderful for them."

"Now you know everything," Bruce replied. "All I need to do now is take a photograph of Becker and the Asian man together. That would be the proof I need to take to Mr. Herbert."

"What can we do to help?" Sarah asked eagerly.

"You can help by staying away from here from now on," Bruce snapped. "Several times I've been close to getting that photo, but then you kids came snooping around and scared the Asian man away."

I knew Sarah was disappointed, but I was more than happy to stay away from spooky woods and isolated farms.

"I'm going to drive you back to town," Bruce announced as he turned on the flashlight he was carrying.

To our surprise, he led us down the hollow on a trail that ran along the stream. After a few minutes the beam from the flashlight picked up something on the other side of the creek.

"Look," I pointed.

Bruce aimed the light and we saw that someone was building a shack out of old boards and logs. A skull and crossbones was painted on the crude door.

□

"Looks like Franklin and his gang are building a secret clubhouse," Sarah chuckled. "I bet that's why they're trying to keep us out of Misty Woods."

The trail finally ended at another spot along Route 19. Bruce's car was parked behind some bushes and he drove us back to town.

"One last thing," he said sternly as he dropped us off at the diner. "Don't talk to *anyone* about this. That includes Conrad Capshaw. This is a top secret operation and you might blow my cover."

Sarah and Frog didn't have much to say as we split up for the night. Sarah was mad because she was kicked off the case. Frog was upset because his hero was a toy spy.

I was the only happy camper. The scary mystery was over for us. I whistled all the way home.

□

20

THE NEXT DAY was Saturday. Even though it was my day off from work, I got up early and headed for the diner. I just can't stay away from the place.

I sat at the counter and Fred McGhee slid me a plate piled high with blueberry pancakes. No sooner did the last delicious bite slide down my throat than Sarah burst into the diner.

"I've been a fool, Lannigan!" she cried, waving her notebook in my face. I noticed she had her camera hanging around her neck.

□

"What *are* you babbling about?" I asked as I calmly wiped my mouth with a napkin.

"I've been thinking about what Bruce told us," she explained. "His story has more holes in it than Franklin O'Grady's brain."

Before I could open my mouth again, she pulled me off the stool.

"Let's go get Frog," she said. "We already might be too late."

We were halfway to the Fenniman house before she began to fill me in.

"Think about it, Lannigan. Bruce told us he's been trying to get a photograph of Dr. Becker and the Asian man together. If that's true, why didn't he have a camera with him last night?"

"Yeah," I said, snapping my fingers. "And we told him we had just seen the Asian man and Dr. Becker go into the barn. Why did he insist on driving us back to town instead of sneaking up to the barn to investigate?"

Sarah nodded as she consulted her notebook.

"I wrote down that we saw Dr. Becker and the Asian man shake hands. Why would Becker want to shake hands with someone who's blackmailing him?"

All kinds of thoughts were now swirling around in my head. We had assumed it was the Asian

□

man we saw trying to break into Dr. Becker's office. But if he and Becker were working together, why would he do such a thing? And if it wasn't the Asian man who attempted the break-in, then who was it?

"I think it was Bruce," Sarah answered firmly.

We found Frog sitting at his card table cutting out pieces of paper for the new, improved Super-Duper Sleuths. We quickly filled him in.

"Yeah," Frog agreed. "And if Too Wonderful really suspected Dr. Becker of stealing its ideas, why wouldn't they just stop letting him into their creative offices? He could demonstrate his toy ideas someplace else."

"And wouldn't they just tell their staff not to share any secret plans with him?" I added.

"When I told Bruce I was going to talk to my grandfather, he made up that whole story to get me to keep quiet," Sarah said angrily. "*And* to get us to stay away from the farm."

"If Bruce *is* the one who's been trying to break into Dr. Becker's office," I chuckled, "we've sure been messing up his plans."

"And we're going to mess him up one last time!" Sarah declared.

"What do you mean?" Frog said.

□

"This might be Bruce's last chance to break in," Sarah explained. "Dr. Becker said he's going to get a guard dog today, and he's already had bars put on all the barn windows."

"Right!" I agreed. "If Bruce doesn't get in today, he'll have to face a guard dog the next time he tries."

"We'd better get out there!" Sarah declared. "Bruce will make his move the minute Dr. Becker leaves to get his dog."

"And speaking of dogs," Frog said. "We'd better take Churchill with us."

"Good idea," Sarah agreed. "We might need that valiant canine."

Churchill had been sleeping under the table. When he heard his name, he trotted out and joined us. He doesn't have much of a tail, so he ends up wagging his whole rear end. Churchill looks short and roly-poly, but as we petted him his body felt hard and muscular.

"C'mon, men," Sarah ordered. "It's time we wrapped this case up once and for all."

"All this trouble over toys," I muttered as we hurried outside. "I thought toys were supposed to be fun."

"Maybe they are, Lannigan," Sarah said. "But from now on we're toying with danger."

□

21

GETTING TO THE farm by way of the woods wasn't easy with Churchill along. He was far more interested in sniffing out every rustling sound in the brush.

"He loves chasing rabbits and squirrels," Frog explained as he tightened his grip on the leash. "Not that he ever catches them."

When we reached the bottom of the hollow, Churchill wanted no part of the swinging bridge. Frog had to pick him up and carry him across. By the time we got to the other side, Frog was wheezing as hard as Churchill.

□

We climbed up out of the hollow and stopped at the edge of the woods. Across the field the farm looked peaceful and deserted.

"I need a volunteer to stay here as lookout," Sarah whispered.

Frog's hand shot up a millionth of a second before mine.

"Use your binoculars and keep a close watch on us," Sarah ordered as she took Churchill's leash from him. "When you see me wave at you, run and call the police. You can probably use one of the phones at the trailer park on Route 19."

Sarah's plan was to take a photograph of Bruce trying to break into Dr. Becker's office. Then she would signal Frog to get help. To get the picture, we would hide in some bushes where we had a clear view of the barn doors.

"He'll have to break into the barn through the doors," Sarah pointed out. "There's no way he can saw his way through those bars over the windows."

Getting to the bushes was the hard part because we had to cross the open field. We tried running as low to the ground as we could. It was easy for Churchill. He was already down there.

We rounded the barn and dove into the bushes that were at the edge of the barnyard. As we

□

crouched down and peered out through the branches, we noticed that Dr. Becker's car was gone.

"He's already left to pick up the guard dog," Sarah whispered. "There should be some action soon."

Nothing happened soon. We watched and waited and fidgeted. Churchill stretched out on the ground and went to sleep.

"Maybe we're too late," Sarah worried. "Maybe Bruce has already been here and gone."

"Or maybe you were just plain wrong about Bruce," I thought to myself.

Suddenly Sarah elbowed me. I followed her gaze to the barn doors. Bruce was creeping around the corner of the barn. The way he kept jerking his head around, it was obvious he was worried about being seen.

Sarah raised her camera to her eye and began snapping pictures as Bruce stopped at the door. He had tools with him and we watched as he began to work on the lock.

"I was right!" Sarah whispered excitedly. "He's trying to break in!"

A few minutes later Bruce pushed the door open and slipped inside. Sarah jumped up and waved toward the woods where Frog was sup-

□

posed to be watching for her signal. Then she hurried toward the barn with Churchill and me close behind.

First, Sarah tried to peek in the door, but Bruce had locked it behind him. We moved around to the side of the barn and looked in a window.

"He's at the back working on the door into Dr. Becker's office," Sarah said. "I wish I could get a picture of him."

"What are you kids doing?" a voice barked at us.

My heart shot to my throat as we spun around. When I recognized the man standing there, it slid back to where it belonged. It was Jerry Nevins, the assistant vice president who had given us the tour of the Too Wonderful Toy Company.

"Mr. Nevins!" I gasped with relief. "I'm glad you're here. Bruce Miller is in the barn trying to break into Dr. Becker's office. Sarah has pictures of him."

Suddenly Nevins reached out and snatched Sarah's camera away from her. With a cry of fury, he smashed it to pieces against the side of the barn.

By now Churchill was growling and pulling at

□

his leash. Sarah quickly leaned over and un-snapped the leash from his collar.

"Churchill!" she yelled. "Attack!"

Like a roly-poly tank, Churchill rumbled forward. I stared in disbelief as he went straight through Mr. Nevins' outstretched legs.

"Churchill!" I shouted as the valiant canine took off across the field after a bounding rabbit. "Come back!"

"Shut up!" Mr. Nevins snapped.

With one smooth motion, he pulled a pistol out of his belt and pointed it at us!

□

22

BRUCE MILLER'S HEAD popped around the corner of the barn.

"What's going on?" he asked in alarm.

"I caught these kids spying on you," Mr. Nevins answered.

"Are you crazy?" Bruce cried. "Why didn't you just leave them alone? It would have been my word against theirs that I was anywhere near this place today. And who's going to believe them? They're just kids!"

"The girl had *pictures* of you, stupid!" Nevins

□

declared, pointing down at the shattered camera.

"I thought I told you kids to butt out!" Bruce yelled.

"Butting in is Sarah's specialty," I muttered.

"Any sign of Wong out there?" Bruce nodded toward the woods.

Mr. Nevins shook his head. "I checked out the whole area. If Wong is anywhere near this place he's invisible."

Mr. Nevins then began pushing us along the side of the barn.

"Let's get on with this," he growled. "We don't know when Becker's coming back."

We followed Bruce into the cool barn while Nevins shut the door behind us.

"How close are you?" Nevins asked.

"Another minute or two and I'll be in," Bruce called from the door at the back of the barn.

"I hope this is worth the risk we're taking!" Mr. Nevins growled.

"Becker said one of the ideas locked in that office is the greatest of his career," Bruce assured him. "He said it just might turn into one of the best-selling toys of all time. That means Majestic will pay us a fortune to find out what it is."

While Bruce worked on the office door, Mr. Nevins leaned back against Frankenstein's table

□

while he kept the pistol pointed at us. Behind him I could see the robot monster lying there as if fast asleep.

"Wake up and help us, Frankie," I thought crazily to myself.

Suddenly the robot's eyes snapped open. I had to swallow a gasp as Frankie began to sit up all by himself. It was as if he had read my desperate thoughts.

It was the humming sound of Frankie's motor that made Mr. Nevins spin around. At first, he just stood there staring in disbelief. Meanwhile, Bruce got the door open in back and hurried through.

"What's going on here?" we heard him shout. "This isn't an office! There's nothing in here but tools!"

By then Frankie was sitting all the way up and reaching his arms toward Mr. Nevins.

"Bruce!" Nevins screamed. "Get back here!"

Sarah was standing next to me, looking down in amazement. When I followed her gaze, I realized that someone was hiding under the table. Suddenly, two hands shot out and grabbed Mr. Nevins' ankles. One strong tug and his feet were yanked out from under him.

With a shriek, Nevins tumbled backward and

□

hit the floor with a thud. Sarah leaped forward and kicked the pistol out of his hand, sending it spinning away. Bruce came charging toward us as the Asian man rolled out from under the table. The Asian man made a lunge for Bruce, but was knocked back down when Bruce gave him a straight-arm in the chest.

By the time Bruce ran out the front door, Mr. Nevins was right behind him and Sarah and I were right behind Mr. Nevins. At first, the two men tried to escape toward the road, but halfway across the barnyard they skidded to a stop. Dr. Becker was blocking their way with an old rusty pitchfork in his hand.

Bruce and Nevins spun around and ran across the field toward the woods. Sarah and I kept on their tails, with the Asian man now joining us. Off to the right I could see Churchill trying to catch up with us, too. He had given up on the rabbit and thought this was a game.

Once Bruce and Mr. Nevins were in the woods, there was only one way to go. Down the path into the hollow. By the time we reached the rim of the hollow, they were running up to the swinging bridge.

"Look on the other side!" I cried when I realized that Frog was standing on the far bank with Franklin O'Grady and his gang.

□

"Frog!" Sarah shouted. "Watch out! Bruce and Nevins are the crooks!"

Suddenly, Frog began to yell orders. The O'Grady gang broke away from him and ran to the four trees where the bridge's ropes were tied.

"They're cutting it down!" Sarah cried. "Let's go!"

As we charged down the path, I could see Franklin and his buddies sawing away at the ropes with their penknives. Mr. Nevins and Bruce were in the middle of the bridge when they realized what was happening. They tried to get across faster, but it was too late. All four ropes snapped at once, and the bridge plunged into the chilly stream, taking Bruce and Mr. Nevins with it.

We reached the bank as the two men popped to the surface, coughing and sputtering.

"Have you two had enough?" the Asian man demanded.

Bruce and Mr. Nevins nodded their heads sadly. The chase was over.

"Excuse me," Sarah said, looking up at the Asian man. "Who are you, anyway?"

"My name's Mike Wong," the man grinned. "And I'm a private detective."

□

23

MORE OF THE mystery was cleared up the next morning. Bruce Miller and Jerry Nevins were in police custody and had confessed everything. Mike Wong, Conrad Capshaw, Sarah, Frog, and I discussed the case over breakfast at the diner. Mr. Wong started out by telling us about his security and investigations business.

"I was born and raised in Pittsburgh," he explained. "Ever since I was a kid I wanted to be a detective."

"Sound familiar?" I chuckled as I poked Sarah.

"I started my agency with one detective. Me! Now I have a staff of twenty."

□

"How did you get on this case?" Sarah asked.

"Mr. Herbert, the president of Too Wonderful, began to suspect that company plans and advertising campaigns were being leaked to the Majestic Toy Company of Boston. Majestic was beating Too Wonderful to the market with knockoff toys. Mr. Herbert decided to hire an outside investigating agency to look into it. Lucky for me that Conrad here suggested mine to him."

"Luck had nothing to do with it," Mr. Capshaw added. "You're one of the best private eyes in the business."

"Working undercover, I came up with a number of possible suspects," Mike went on. "Bruce Miller was one of them. Eventually, I ruled out everyone but him. I was positive that Miller was the source of the leaks."

"What about Jerry Nevins?" Sarah asked.

"Mr. Herbert was convinced that Bruce wasn't acting alone. He was sure someone higher up in the company was also involved. Someone who had access to all parts of Too Wonderful's operations. I began to secretly follow Bruce, hoping he would lead me to the bigger fish."

"Is that what you were doing when we kept running into you in Misty Woods?" Sarah asked. "Tailing Bruce?"

"Right," Mike nodded. "At first, I couldn't

figure out why he was sneaking around those woods at night. But as I learned more about Grady Becker, I realized that Bruce wanted to steal ideas from him, *too*."

"So it *was* Bruce we saw trying to break into Dr. Becker's office that night," I said. "We thought it was you, and we told Bruce."

"You sure blew my cover," Mike pointed out. "Bruce told Jerry Nevins, and they put two and two together. They knew an investigation was underway, and Nevins managed to find out that my agency was involved."

"They must have known that time was running out on them," Sarah remarked.

"Lucky for our case they were greedy," Mike Wong agreed. "Even though they knew Bruce was under suspicion and being followed, they still couldn't resist trying to get at Dr. Becker's secret ideas and plans. It was their downfall. Up until then I still didn't have much hard evidence against Bruce, and I didn't even know that Nevins was the other person in it with him."

"When did Dr. Becker get involved?" Sarah asked.

"I filled him in after the first break-in attempt. We then met several times to work out a trap. Becker told Bruce he was going to get a guard dog on Saturday. I figured that Bruce and his

□

mystery friend would try and break in while Becker was gone."

"If Dr. Becker was supposed to go get the dog," Sarah wondered, "what was he doing at the farm chasing Bruce and Mr. Nevins with a pitchfork?"

Mike chuckled. "The guard dog story was just a trick to push Bruce and his friend into action. I wanted Dr. Becker to leave the area during my stakeout, but he insisted on sticking around to back me up."

"Speaking of stakeouts," Sarah said, "what were you doing hiding under Frankenstein's table?"

"It was Becker's idea that I wait for the thieves *inside* the barn. Under the table seemed like a good place to hide."

"It was great the way you used Frankie to get the drop on Mr. Nevins," I remarked.

"Dr. Becker had showed me how he worked during our last meeting," Mike laughed. "I never thought it would come in handy."

"I still can't believe we thought you were guilty," I said.

"Yeah," Frog giggled. "We sure had the *Wong* man!"

Everyone groaned and then laughed.

□

24

AFTER BREAKFAST Sarah, Frog, and I headed out to Dr. Becker's. The inventor wanted to thank us personally for helping on the case. Of course, we couldn't use the path to get there because the swinging bridge was down.

As we walked out Misty Hollow Road, Frog had to tell us again about his part in the capture. While we were hiding in the bushes, he had been watching us through his binoculars. Suddenly he noticed Mr. Nevins creeping toward the barn. He had been so busy watching Nevins that he missed Sarah's signal to call the police.

☐

"But when I saw him pull that pistol on you, I knew it was time to get help," he declared.

Frog had run down into the hollow and crossed the bridge. No sooner did he reach the other side than Franklin O'Grady and his gang took him prisoner.

"We were right about that shack," Frog pointed out. "It's their secret hideout and they thought we were hanging around the woods trying to find it."

"As if we cared," Sarah sniffed.

"I tried to tell them the truth about what was going on, but they thought I was lying," Frog went on. "Not until they saw Mr. Nevins and Bruce being chased by you guys did they believe me."

"And then they were only too glad to give someone else a dunking," I added.

"I guess I owe them one," Sarah said sadly.

When we got to the farm, we found Dr. Becker in the barn putting the finishing touches on Frankie.

"The Pennywood Park people will be picking him up tomorrow," the inventor told us. "I'll miss him, but I guess I can always visit him in his new Haunted House Horrors home."

□

Sarah walked over to a worktable and picked up a pistol that was lying there.

"This is Mr. Nevins' gun," she declared.

"Look at the bottom of the handle," Dr. Becker said.

Sarah turned the pistol over and gasped.

"It says Majestic Toy Company!" she exclaimed. "It's a toy gun!"

"Many children are seriously hurt every year because they're carrying toy guns like this and people think they are real," Dr. Becker said bitterly. "That's one reason I quit working for Majestic and became an independent."

"Why did Bruce and Mr. Nevins do it?" I wondered.

"They did it for money," Dr. Becker said angrily. "Majestic paid them well for each piece of information they smuggled out. They were also promised high-paying jobs at Majestic whenever they quit Too Wonderful."

"They sure made a clever team," Sarah commented.

"It was Bruce's idea to turn spy," Dr. Becker explained. "But he needed someone higher up at Too Wonderful to help him. Someone who was closer to all the company ideas and plans and projects."

□

"So Bruce recruited Jerry Nevins, an assistant vice president," Sarah added.

"What about your office?" Frog asked. "We heard Bruce yell out that there wasn't anything back there but tools."

"Do you think I'd be stupid enough to tell everybody I keep top secret toy ideas and plans locked in that room if I really did?" Dr. Becker snorted. "That toolroom is my decoy."

"You sure had us fooled," I admitted.

"And Bruce, too," Dr. Becker chuckled.

"Where *do* you keep your ideas and plans hidden?" Frog asked.

"Have you forgotten what I told you? If you're going to be a successful toy inventor, you have to keep your ideas a secret for as long as you can. If I told you where I keep mine hidden, they wouldn't be hidden anymore, would they?"

Dr. Becker then handed each of us an envelope containing a hundred dollar bill.

"Maybe you can use your reward to buy a new camera," he said to Sarah.

"And I'll use mine to make the new, improved Super-Duper Sleuths," Frog exclaimed. "Then I'll show it to you."

"Very good," Dr. Becker replied. "And now

□

you'll have to excuse me. I have a new project to get started on."

"I'm sure looking forward to getting back to work on my game," Frog declared as we walked back to town.

"And I'm looking forward to spending the rest of the summer with no scary mysteries to solve," I said, staring hard at Sarah so she'd get the point.

But Sarah had a strange look on her face.

"Don't count on it, Lannigan," she said mysteriously. "Don't count on it."